# LUCINDA WICKED

# Nail Me Down

*Copyright © 2025 by Lucinda Wicked*

*All rights reserved. No part of this publication may be reproduced, stored or transmitted in any form or by any means, electronic, mechanical, photocopying, recording, scanning, or otherwise without written permission from the publisher. It is illegal to copy this book, post it to a website, or distribute it by any other means without permission.*

*This novel is entirely a work of fiction. The names, characters and incidents portrayed in it are the work of the author's imagination. Any resemblance to actual persons, living or dead, events or localities is entirely coincidental.*

*Lucinda Wicked asserts the moral right to be identified as the author of this work.*

*Lucinda Wicked has no responsibility for the persistence or accuracy of URLs for external or third-party Internet Websites referred to in this publication and does not guarantee that any content on such Websites is, or will remain, accurate or appropriate.*

*Designations used by companies to distinguish their products are often claimed as trademarks. All brand names and product names used in this book and on its cover are trade names, service marks, trademarks and registered trademarks of their respective owners. The publishers and the book are not associated with any product or vendor mentioned in this book. None of the companies referenced within the book have endorsed the book.*

*First edition*

*This book was professionally typeset on Reedsy.
Find out more at reedsy.com*

## Contents

| | |
|---|---|
| *Pronunciation Guide for Nail Me Down* | iv |
| Chapter 1: Stilettos on Concrete | 1 |
| Chapter 2: Softcore Streamer, Hardcore Problem | 8 |
| Chapter 3: Blueprints and Boundary Lines | 13 |
| Chapter 4: Power Outage | 18 |
| Chapter 5: Respawn | 25 |
| Chapter 6: Kitchen Quiet, Streaming Loud | 33 |
| Chapter 7: Load-Bearing Tension | 39 |
| Chapter 8: Ghosts Don't Bring Flowers | 46 |
| Chapter 9: Pixel Kinks | 52 |
| Chapter 10: Fallout | 60 |
| Chapter 11: Patch Notes | 66 |
| Chapter 12: Velvet Leash | 72 |
| Chapter 13: Final Walkthrough | 80 |
| Chapter 14: Soft Reset | 88 |
| Chapter 15: Hard Hat Heart | 95 |
| Epilogue – Glitched and Glorious | 102 |

# Pronunciation Guide for Nail Me Down

*Character Names*

- **Maeve Kincaid** – /māv kin-KADE/
- *Maeve*: rhymes with "wave"
- *Kincaid*: stress on the second syllable
- **Orly "Lolo" Stavrou** – /OR-lee "LOH-loh" stav-ROO/
- *Orly*: like "or" + "lee"
- *Lolo*: low-low (equal emphasis on both syllables)
- *Stavrou*: stress on the second syllable; rhymes with "crew"

Other Key Terms

- **UX Design** – /yoo-eks dɪ-ZAHYN/
- Acronym for "User Experience Design"
- **Dreamlight Valley** – /DREEM-lite VAL-ee/

# Chapter 1: Stilettos on Concrete

Maeve Kincaid lived in order, steel, and silence. Her life ran on schedule. boots laced before dawn, calloused hands scribbling measurements before the sun cleared the scaffolding, and a clipboard she wielded like a blade. She didn't do glitter. She didn't do perfume, and she most certainly didn't do people who thought they could coast on charisma instead of concrete.

The site that morning was a gutted shell of what would become a luxury wellness retreat—glass, stone, subtle lighting, and enough money sunk into the floors to make even Maeve's seasoned crew nervous. They didn't say it out loud, but she could feel it in the way they held their tools tighter than usual. Wellness. That always meant two things: clients who spoke in words like "flow" and "vibration" and chaos wearing a clipboard.

What no one expected, however, was for chaos to walk in wearing velvet boots.

## Nail Me Down

Orly Stavrou—called Lolo by some, whispered about already by others—was five foot five, maybe, but filled every inch of the construction site like smoke. Her curves were unapologetic, midsized, and decadent in a way that pulled the air taut. Her blouse, black mesh and soft enough to flutter, clung over full breasts and a plush belly that suggested she didn't shy away from pleasure. Her curls, streaked with caramel, were clipped back with a silver claw that looked more like a weapon than an accessory. Her mouth, painted the color of dried blood, curved easily. Too easily.

It took her ninety seconds to command the crew's attention.

"This the site lead?" she asked, glancing at Maeve without hesitation, already knowing the answer. Her tone was low and smooth, measured confidence, not arrogance. She was used to rooms reacting to her. even when those rooms were made of dust and drywall.

Maeve's jaw ticked. "Yeah. You with our suppliers?"

"UX design," Lolo replied, eyes already roaming the unfinished beams. "Wellness client brought me in to optimize user flow through the space. Lobby. Gym. Emotional navigation through structure." She said it like it made perfect sense. As if steel beams and spa chakras had always belonged in the same sentence.

The crew looked between them, silent. Suspicious. Entertained.

Maeve said nothing for a beat too long, her silence heavy. Then, flatly: "Flow. Right."

## Chapter 1: Stilettos on Concrete

Lolo smiled. Not politely. She extended a hand, manicured with black polish sharp enough to slice. "Orly Stavrou. Most people call me Lolo."

Maeve didn't shake it.

"We're still pouring concrete in the east wing," Maeve said. "Hope flow includes avoiding trip hazards."

Lolo's smirk deepened, not the least bit offended. "Is that a threat," she asked, tilting her head, "or just flirtation?"

She walked past Maeve then, hips swaying with deliberate ease, curls bouncing with each step like punctuation marks. The silence from the crew fractured; someone coughed. Someone else muttered a quiet 'fuck'.

Lolo didn't pause to bask in it. She already had what she needed. Not just access to the job site, but attention. Gravity. The unspoken question was no longer who she is, but how the hell is she still walking in those boots without breaking her neck on exposed tile?

Maeve followed. Of course she did. Pretending it was to make sure the consultant didn't trip over rebar. Pretending it had nothing to do with the tight pull behind her sternum or the way Lolo's perfume—patchouli, citrus, and something darker, aged in shadows—hung behind her like a promise someone wasn't brave enough to say out loud.

In front of the half-framed atrium, Lolo paused. She turned a slow circle, tablet in hand, already sketching invisible changes into the air.

"You're going to want more light," she said. "The space reads too cold. Linear symmetry is fine for an office, but this is a place people are supposed to breathe. Right now, it feels like a corridor leading to judgment."

Maeve frowned. "The layout's approved."

"Sure," Lolo said, barely looking up. "But so were open-plan offices. We all know how that ended."

The silence crackled.

Maeve didn't argue—not because she agreed, but because the fire in her chest didn't come from logic. It came from something else. Something dangerously close to intrigue.

"You don't have a thing for softness, huh?" Lolo asked, eyes dragging over her slowly, deliberately.

It wasn't a question. It was a provocation.

Maeve didn't answer. She couldn't. Not with the way Lolo stood there, framed by unfinished beams like a contradiction built into flesh. She was softness with teeth. Curves that refused shame. The kind of woman who looked like she owned the words 'too much' and wore them like jewelry.

"You're going to be in the way," Maeve said finally.

## Chapter 1: Stilettos on Concrete

Lolo didn't flinch. She only smiled. "Then you'll just have to move around me."

She left Maeve standing there, breath shallow, pulse irregular. It was unclear if she knew what she'd done—or if that was just how she walked through the world. Like desire was an atmosphere. Structure bent to her anyway.

Maeve should've ignored her. Should've buried herself back in floorplans and steel orders. But Lolo kept showing up. Always in dark layers and tight silhouettes, always with a new observation that felt less like a suggestion and more like a dare. She pointed out ceiling height disparities in the yoga room. She questioned the placement of electrical outlets like she'd been born in blueprints. She offered criticism with compliments laced between the lines: "I can tell you've got a good eye for angles. But what about rhythm?"

Maeve hated that the question stayed with her. Hated it more when she caught herself staring at Lolo's lips during a walk-through. At the gentle swell of her belly. The way she leaned into softness like it was a language only she had mastered.

Then, there was the morning on the scaffold.

Lolo was already up there when Maeve arrived—balanced high above the atrium, curls tied back with black ribbon, the sharp curve of her thigh visible through slit pants as she adjusted a digital layout on her tablet. One of the crew stood beside her, holding the rail.

Maeve barely swallowed a growl. "You're not cleared for scaffold work."

"I am now," Lolo called down. "Site manager signed off. Besides, I'm not working—I'm looking."

"At what?"

"Sight lines. The client wants a meditative transition corridor. Something that makes the chaos stop at the door. Visual design leads emotional flow. You want stillness? You have to build for it."

Maeve stared.

Lolo tilted her head, innocent. "People think UX is about screens. It's about control. You of all people should appreciate that."

The words hit harder than they should have. Control. As if that's what Maeve was made of—steel bones and nothing else.

Maeve crossed her arms. "You always talk like you're narrating a TED Talk?"

"Only when people look like they're trying not to punch a wall."

For the first time, Maeve almost smiled.

Lolo noticed.

## Chapter 1: Stilettos on Concrete

There, in the scaffolding dust, with sun through rafters and half the crew pretending not to eavesdrop, something shifted. Not loudly. But irrevocably.

Lolo descended the scaffold. Boots still unscuffed. She paused just long enough beside Maeve to murmur, "You think I'm just here to annoy you."

"You're succeeding."

"But you're still watching."

Maeve didn't answer. She didn't need to.

She walked away.

Lolo—self-assured and sharp-eyed—let her. No gloating. No smirk. Just the quiet, satisfied air of someone who had already mapped out the blueprints of something inevitable.

Maeve returned to her board, her notes, her clipboard. Pretending the air didn't still taste like heat. Pretending she wasn't calculating the safest way to build around a woman who clearly had no interest in being avoided.

Some things weren't meant to be designed. They were meant to be demolished first. Then rebuilt—one sharp breath at a time.

# Chapter 2: Softcore Streamer, Hardcore Problem

Maeve didn't bring her work home so much as she built her home out of work. Her loft was all exposed brick and steel bones, a gutted old industrial unit she'd renovated herself, one beam and busted nail at a time. There were still traces of it in the air—sawdust sealed into the floorboards, faint oil in the grain of the wood, the kind of quiet that echoed only when you were alone too long. Maeve didn't keep plants. She didn't keep people either. Just a heavy workbench that doubled as a dining table, a mattress on a handmade platform frame, and a dual-monitor setup that glowed violet in the corner of her living space. Her one indulgence, a top-of-the-line gaming rig, quietly overbuilt and never talked about.

She'd meant to keep working that night. Blueprints were spread across the table. Her fingers hovered over her stylus, not

## Chapter 2: Softcore Streamer, Hardcore Problem

drawing, just pressing it into the pad as if force could summon focus. But her eyes weren't on the screen anymore. They were on her phone. On the little bubble that had popped up from a random Instagram scroll: LoloStav—Live on Twitch.

It was curiosity. Just that. Curiosity and mild workplace surveillance. Maeve clicked it open.

The screen loaded, and the lighting hit first—soft pinks and candle-glow gold, shadows dancing in the corners of the frame. The camera was angled just enough to show a plush velvet chair, a gaming desk littered with crystals and enamel pins, and Lolo herself, curled into the scene like she belonged there more than most people belonged anywhere. She was in full cosplay—black wings tucked back, green velvet corset clinging to her like ivy, thigh-highs just visible above the edge of the desk. Gothic Tinkerbell, Maeve thought. Then hated herself a little for the accuracy.

The audio kicked in. Lolo's voice, the same one Maeve had been pretending not to hear in her sleep, purred through the stream like it was wired directly into her spine. "We're back in Dreamlight tonight," she said, voice low and syrupy. "I've got pumpkins to harvest and zero patience for Scrooge McDuck's bullshit economy. Also," she paused dramatically, smile creeping, "this one's for my favorite forearms in flannel."

Maeve froze.

The chat exploded with comments. Some laughing, some thirsty, most supportive in a way that annoyed Maeve for reasons she didn't care to name. She stared at the screen. At Lolo's smirk. The casual way she tucked a dark curl behind her ear and tilted her head like she hadn't just sent a slow-burning missile across Maeve's gut.

She didn't close the stream.

She should have. Instead, she adjusted the volume. Sat back. And watched.

Lolo played the game with surprising skill. There was a rhythm to it: planting, harvesting, decorating her little digital village with gothic archways and cobblestone paths. Occasionally, she would switch accents midstream—French, vaguely Southern, sometimes British when narrating a villain's line. Maeve didn't smile. But her mouth softened.

There was a moment—an offhanded one—when Lolo leaned forward to grab something off-camera, and the neckline of her corset shifted. Just slightly. Enough to catch Maeve's attention. Enough to make her notice the softness of the belly beneath, the curve of her waist, the way her body moved like it was built to be worshipped slowly. Not perfect. Not plastic. Real. Tangible. Completely, unapologetically hers.

Maeve looked away.

She tried to go back to her blueprints. She stared at a load-bearing crossbeam for ten straight minutes and couldn't remember what she was supposed to be adjusting. Her hand gripped the stylus tighter. She opened a browser window and

## *Chapter 2: Softcore Streamer, Hardcore Problem*

typed "UX design spatial layout certifications" just to feel like she was doing something productive. She found nothing useful. Closed the tab. Returned to the stream.

Now Lolo was humming—soft, tuneless, something half-familiar and lullaby-sweet. Her camera had zoomed slightly, just enough to show her gaming hands. Short nails, silver rings, bracelets with tiny charms that jingled when she clicked through menus. Maeve couldn't look away. Not because it was sexual—not entirely—but because it was intimate. Because it was hers, this version of Lolo no one at the job site had seen. No smirks. No verbal sparring. Just light, and laughter, and a woman who clearly loved building things, even if they were made of pixels.

Maeve's jaw clenched again. Her hand, unconsciously, moved to her phone. She thumbed the stream chat open. Typed half a message. Deleted it. Typed again.

**AnonymousUser44:** Nice setup.

Lolo's head lifted slightly, like a cat catching a scent. She squinted at her monitor. "Hmm," she said aloud. "Is that you, boss lady? I can smell you in here."

Maeve's face flushed instantly. She muted the stream. Closed the window.

Turned off the monitors.

Stood up.

## Nail Me Down

Paced.

She told herself it was nothing. Just a weird, voyeuristic fluke. A momentary lapse.

But the truth was Lolo had caught her. Not just on stream. Not just at work. She'd threaded herself under Maeve's skin in ways no one ever had. Maeve had always kept her boundaries neat—blueprinted, reinforced, finished with trim and sealant. No one got in. If they did, they didn't stay.

But Lolo? Lolo had cracked something open and left it there. Smiling. Streaming. Knowing.

Maeve returned to her work table. She didn't open the plans. She sat. Folded her hands.

She wondered if she'd just lost control of her own build.

# Chapter 3: Blueprints and Boundary Lines

By the time the concrete cured on the south wall, the boundary lines between Maeve's job site and Lolo's presence on it had already started to erode.

It wasn't dramatic. That wasn't Lolo's style. She didn't throw tantrums or challenge authority with the kind of self-righteous entitlement Maeve was used to shutting down. No—Lolo infiltrated. Quietly. Elegantly. With a confident smile and language that sounded like it had been plucked from a meditation retreat brochure, all while she stood in a mesh top and leather pencil skirt sharp enough to slice drywall.

She didn't belong on a site like this. Not really. Yet she moved through it like she'd been cast in the blueprint from day one. Maeve had seen consultants fumble through construction zones before, all nervous glances and clipped apologies, but not Lolo.

Lolo navigated the raw skeleton of the building like she was hosting a gallery walk. Like every exposed beam and roll of wire was just another curated aesthetic for her to critique, and she critiqued everything.

"This corner reads like emotional gridlock," she'd said once, gesturing at a section of the unfinished second floor.

Maeve hadn't even looked up from her clipboard. "It reads like a hallway."

"A hallway," Lolo echoed, tapping a red-polished nail against her tablet, "that makes people feel like they're late for something."

"You're late for a hard hat," Maeve had shot back.

But the words had lacked venom. There was no real heat to it. Not anymore. Just friction—the kind that sparked slowly, dangerously, until everything started to burn.

Maeve tried to stay focused. She paced the job site like a drill sergeant, barking orders and rerouting her crew, triple-checking installations like her life depended on it. Because maybe it did. Because if she stopped moving, she might start watching again. Watching the way Lolo lingered when she spoke. Watching the subtle shift in her hips when she leaned over a digital model on her tablet, hips Maeve had already dreamed about once, maybe twice—dreams she refused to acknowledge in daylight.

So when Lolo brushed past her that morning—deliberately,

## Chapter 3: Blueprints and Boundary Lines

slowly, with a whisper of her perfume trailing behind—it wasn't surprising that Maeve reacted. What was surprising was how visibly.

"You've got to stop getting underfoot," she said, voice low, sharp, but already fraying at the edges.

Lolo didn't even look at her. Just smirked, tucking her tablet under one arm and stepping closer instead of away. Close enough that Maeve could see the faint sheen of sweat at her collarbone. Close enough that she could feel the warmth of her body radiating through the chill in the concrete.

"Maybe if you had clearer paths," Lolo murmured, "I wouldn't keep getting in the way."

Maeve narrowed her eyes. "We're not in a game, Stavrou."

"You sure?" Lolo tilted her head, curls spilling over one shoulder. "Because you keep acting like I'm playing one you don't know the rules to."

Maeve didn't reply. Didn't move. She couldn't. Her jaw was locked, and her fists were clenched, and if she opened her mouth, she wasn't sure what would come out—orders or pleas or something so hungry it would make the air taste different.

She turned on her heel and walked away. Her boots echoed down the hallway louder than they needed to.

That should've been the end of it. Another skirmish in a war they both pretended wasn't happening.

But later that night, after Maeve had showered and redlined corrections into three separate floorplans, her phone buzzed.

One message. One image.

Lolo, in front of a mirror. Black corset, thigh-high stockings. Her curls down, wild. Her lips parted just enough to ruin a man. Or a woman with a hammer and no self-control. The caption was short.

Too much?

Maeve stared at it too long. Not blinking. Not breathing.

Then she set her jaw, snapped a photo of the project's current blueprint—dead center, the words EAST CORRIDOR WALL SHIFTED 12.5 CM FOR FLOWLINE circled in red—and replied with one word.

Definitely.

Then she turned her phone off.

She didn't see the poll Lolo posted a few minutes later on her Twitch stream.

"Do you think she wants to pin me to a wall or pretend I don't exist?"

## Chapter 3: Blueprints and Boundary Lines

The results were decisive:
*92%: Both.*

Maeve didn't need to see the numbers. She already knew them. She could feel them in the heat she hadn't been able to shake since that morning. In the dreams that had started shifting from vague outlines to detailed maps of Lolo's mouth. In the way she'd started avoiding eye contact, because every time she made it, Lolo looked back with no fear. Only invitation.

The worst part? Maeve was beginning to understand that the blueprint she kept drawing might never be enough to keep Lolo out.

Lolo wasn't trying to bulldoze her walls. She was reworking them from the inside.

She wasn't breaking boundaries. She was redrawing them.

Maeve was the one letting her do it.

## Chapter 4: Power Outage

The storm rolled in without warning, the sky over the site turning from slate to obsidian in a matter of minutes. One of the crew called out about the wind picking up. Another pointed to a cluster of clouds that looked more like bruises than weather. Maeve didn't stop working. She just muttered about deadlines and city permits and snapped her pencil when the power cut with a hard, mechanical thunk. The site fell into silence. Machinery powered down, lights blinked off. The only sound was the rain starting to tap against the temporary skylights and the muttered curses of half a dozen electricians caught mid-install.

Lolo was in the lobby, tablet dead, staring at the nearest window like she was enjoying the view. She didn't seem surprised. Of course she didn't. If Maeve had to guess, Lolo had probably predicted this storm two days ago, planned her wardrobe accordingly, and smiled through the entire thing just to see if Maeve would crack.

## Chapter 4: Power Outage

"You'll want to get off-site before it floods," Maeve said, approaching with tension wound so tight her voice nearly trembled from it. "Transformers on this block are ancient. Grid'll be down for hours."

Lolo turned, slow, the kind of turn people wrote songs about. She was in a long black coat today, leather-trimmed, collar popped against the wind. Underneath, a black dress that clung to her like it had been poured on. Her curls were pinned up messily, a few dark strands falling against her neck. "Are you offering me a ride?" she asked, one brow arched in amusement.

Maeve wanted to say no. She really, truly did. But what came out was: "I'm not letting you wait for a Lyft in this mess."

Lolo didn't say thank you. She just followed her to the truck with that same quiet confidence she always carried, like she knew exactly what this was and exactly where it was going. The silence between them as they drove was thick enough to crack. Rain hammered the windshield. The wipers squeaked against the glass. Lolo didn't touch the radio. Maeve didn't speak.

She pulled into her building's garage, led Lolo upstairs without explaining why she had a keyless entry but no doormat, why the hall smelled like old cedar and something more feral, more lived-in. When the door opened, Maeve stepped aside, let Lolo in first.

The loft was dark, but the power here still held. Bare Edison bulbs hung from a repurposed beam, casting gold light over concrete floors and matte black walls. The entire space was open—workbench, gaming setup, exposed pipes, and a single large bed tucked into the corner with no headboard and no art above it. No clutter. Just muscle and shadow. Just control.

Lolo turned slowly, her voice hushed now, lower. "This feels… very you."

Maeve didn't respond.

Lolo took a few steps deeper, shrugging off her coat, revealing more of the dress underneath. It was clingy, ribbed velvet, low-cut and high-hemmed, stopping just at the tops of her thick thighs. She had no business looking that good after walking through a construction zone. Her makeup hadn't even smudged. "You're not going to offer me coffee?" she asked, teasing.

Maeve stared at her. Hard. "No."

That word cracked the moment wide open.

Lolo took a step forward. Another. The air between them buzzed like a pulled wire.

"You're staring," she said softly.

"You planned that outfit."

"You like it."

Silence.

## Chapter 4: Power Outage

Then Maeve moved.

She didn't lean in gently. She didn't ask for permission with her eyes. She stepped forward, wrapped one hand around Lolo's waist, and the other around the back of her neck, pulling her in fast and hard and angry. Their mouths met like flint striking steel, the kiss all teeth and heat and years of tension compacted into a single explosion. Lolo gasped against her lips but didn't pull back. She surged into it, pressing against Maeve's frame with the kind of want that left no room for hesitation.

Maeve spun her, hard enough to make Lolo's back hit the wall with a thud. Concrete. Cold. Lolo arched into it anyway, letting out a breathy little laugh that turned into a moan when Maeve gripped her thigh and hitched her leg up.

"You're a menace," Maeve growled against her throat, kissing, biting, breathing her in like she was oxygen laced with danger.

"You like that about me," Lolo whispered, her voice thick with sugar and smugness, curling into Maeve like temptation wrapped in silk.

Maeve didn't respond. She pressed her thigh between Lolo's legs and dragged it upward, slow and hard. Lolo choked on a gasp—sharp, involuntary—her body arching, grinding instinctively. Her dress had bunched high above her hips, baring the soft crease where her thighs met. She was already spreading, already wet through her panties, and Maeve could feel the heat of it seeping through the fabric.

## Nail Me Down

With one hand, Maeve pinned Lolo by the throat—not tight, just enough to keep her still, to make her look her in the eye. The other hand dragged up Lolo's thigh and disappeared beneath the hem. Her fingers curled around the soaked elastic, tugging it aside with a practiced flick.

"You walk around that site like you own it," Maeve muttered darkly, her breath brushing the shell of Lolo's ear. "Like I won't fuck the smug out of you."

"I'm untouchable," Lolo gasped, defiant even as her back arched off the wall. "Or I was—until now."

Maeve's fingers found her.

Slick. Hot. Needy.

"Fuck," Maeve hissed, eyes flicking down.

Lolo smirked, her voice wrecked and breathless. "Told you."

Maeve didn't reply. She just pushed two fingers in—slow, deep, curling up until Lolo's head hit the wall with a soft thud. Lolo whimpered, her hands clawing at Maeve's arms now, the confidence melting from her limbs.

"That's it," Maeve murmured. "Come apart for me."

She pumped her fingers slow at first, working Lolo open while her thumb rolled firm, steady circles over her clit. Lolo was panting now, lips parted, neck arched, her whole body

## Chapter 4: Power Outage

trembling against the wall. Maeve watched every twitch, every flutter of Lolo's belly, the stutter of her thighs.

"You think I don't see how you look at me on site?" Maeve growled. "You think you can tease me all day, and I won't take what's mine the second we're alone?"

Lolo cried out—sharp, cracked, half-hiccuped.

Maeve withdrew, fast. Lolo whined, legs buckling slightly.

Before she could complain, Maeve grabbed her by the waist, spun her around, and bent her forward—chest to wall, dress bunched to her hips, panties still askew.

"No," Maeve said low into her ear, voice rough. "This isn't a warning."

She shoved her hand between Lolo's thighs again and thrust her fingers in deep, fucking her without mercy. Her other hand pinned Lolo's wrists above her head. Lolo's mouth fell open, but no sound came. Just a ragged moan, breathless and broken.

The rhythm built fast—wet, desperate, primal.

Lolo came hard, legs shaking, gasping Maeve's name like it hurt to say it. But she didn't stop. Maeve fucked her through it, fingers relentless, until Lolo was whimpering, laughing, sobbing, "More. Please, I need—fuck—I need—"

Maeve curled her fingers just right and whispered, "Then take it."

Lolo came again—screaming this time.

When it was over, when her knees gave out and Maeve caught her, they collapsed onto the mattress in a tangled heap. Lolo's dress was still hitched at her waist, and Maeve's shirt was soaked with sweat. Neither of them spoke. Just the sound of Lolo's ragged breathing and Maeve's hand stroking her thigh—grounding her, claiming her all over again.

"You're not as cold as you pretend," Lolo murmured after a long silence, lips brushing Maeve's collarbone.

Maeve didn't reply. But her hand found Lolo's thigh and stayed there.

The storm outside cracked like an omen.

Inside, nothing was silent anymore.

## Chapter 5: Respawn

The loft still smelled like rain and sweat and sex. The storm hadn't passed, not entirely. Morning light spilled in through half-closed blinds, casting streaks across bare concrete and exposed steel. The air was still heavy with electricity, like the room itself hadn't stopped crackling since last night.

Maeve had woken early, as always, but for once, she hadn't gotten up.

She sat propped against the headboard—what passed for one, anyway; a slab of polished salvage wood she'd bolted to the wall herself—watching the woman still tangled in her sheets like a siren in someone else's bed. Orly "Lolo" Stavrou was all soft angles and intentional chaos. Curled up in nothing but Maeve's favorite flannel, the red-and-black one with the worn collar and the smell of sawdust still stitched into the seams. The shirt was too big for her and somehow perfect. It clung loose over her chest, hitched high on her thighs, open just enough to show the curve of her belly and the faint bruises Maeve had left along her hips.

Lolo didn't seem to care about modesty. She was too busy playing Dreamlight Valley on her Switch, nestled under a chunky knit blanket like she hadn't been wrecked against a wall the night before. Her legs were spread carelessly, toes wiggling, and her thick curls had fallen out of whatever clips had been holding them up. A few stuck to her cheek. She didn't brush them away.

Maeve watched her play without saying anything. She didn't need to.

Lolo knew she was awake. Had known for a while.

She just hadn't looked up yet.

Which made it worse.

Maeve's jaw tightened. Her fingers flexed against her thigh. She counted the beats of her patience and lost track around six.

Lolo let out a soft hum, exaggerated in the way only a brat looking for trouble could get away with. "Morning," she said lightly, still not glancing away from the screen.

Maeve didn't answer.

"I harvested all my pumpkins," Lolo went on, clicking something

## Chapter 5: Respawn

with a dramatic little flourish of her fingers. "Also, I unlocked the evil queen's throne room. It's extremely on-brand."

Maeve exhaled once, slow. Controlled. "You're playing Dreamlight Valley," she said flatly.

Lolo finally looked up. Her expression was pure mischief. "You say that like it's not sacred."

Maeve's eyes dropped, slowly, to where Lolo sat curled under the blanket, legs sprawled wide. The flannel had ridden up—her thighs bare, her panties barely visible beneath the hem. Her fingers moved across the Switch's controls, but her gaze kept flicking toward Maeve like she was waiting for consequences.

"You say that like you're not trying to distract me," Maeve said, voice still thick with sleep, but no less sharp.

Lolo's lips curled. "Am I?"

Maeve moved in a single, deliberate shift—off the headboard, onto her knees, then across the mattress with the kind of slow precision that made Lolo's thighs clench. She didn't rush. Didn't need to. She was inevitable, and Lolo knew it. She stood like prey that wanted to be caught.

Maeve reached out and flicked the Switch off with one finger.

Lolo gasped. "I was—"

"Kneel."

## Nail Me Down

The word landed like an anchor.

Lolo blinked, then narrowed her eyes, trying to play it cool. But Maeve simply raised one brow—calm, certain, unmoved.

Lolo swallowed, cheeks pinking. She set the Switch aside and slid off the bed, blanket trailing behind her. She knelt between Maeve's legs with exaggerated slowness, eyes glinting with mischief. Her posture was perfect: back straight, thighs spread, her lips parted in something just shy of a smirk. The flannel gaped at her chest, showing the slope of her breasts, her nipples hard from cool air and anticipation.

Maeve let the silence stretch until the air around them grew hot and still.

"You want my attention?" she asked, her voice like rough velvet. "Ask for it."

Lolo tilted her head, bratty and beautiful. "You're the one who woke up staring."

Maeve moved fast—fingers curling around Lolo's jaw, tilting her chin up. "Don't make me repeat myself."

Something shifted in Lolo's face. That delicious flicker—defiance folding into need. Her lashes fluttered. Her thighs trembled slightly, but she didn't break eye contact.

"Please," she whispered. Then again, louder, her breath catching. "Please. Pay attention to me."

## Chapter 5: Respawn

Maeve's grip softened. She brushed her thumb along Lolo's cheekbone and murmured, "Good girl."

That did it—Lolo's breath hitched, her entire body leaning forward like praise itself unraveled her.

Maeve slid her hand beneath the flannel, dragging her palm across Lolo's soft belly. She lingered there, just to feel the way Lolo quivered beneath her touch. Then her fingers dipped lower, teasing the waistband of her panties, dragging the pads of her fingers across warm, tender skin.

"You're still sore, aren't you?" Maeve asked, voice soft but sure.

Lolo nodded quickly, eyes glassy. "Yes."

"You want more anyway."

Another nod. "Please."

Maeve pushed her hand between Lolo's legs and found her already soaked. The heat of her, the need—she pulsed against Maeve's fingers, hips already twitching forward.

"You brat your way into my lap, wear my flannel like you want to be claimed, and think I won't notice?"

Lolo moaned, desperate now. "Maybe."

Maeve grinned, wicked and slow. "Wrong answer."

She hooked her fingers, angled them just right, and drove them in deep.

Lolo's entire body jerked forward, forehead dropping to Maeve's thigh as a strangled moan escaped her lips.

"Try again," Maeve said, curling her fingers, stroking slow and firm.

"I wanted—" Lolo gasped, words tangled in the sound of her own breathing. "I wanted you to touch me."

Maeve's hand didn't slow. "Much better."

She pumped her fingers with purpose now—each thrust deliberate, each drag designed to find every weak spot inside her. Her thumb pressed tight against Lolo's clit, grinding small circles in a rhythm that stole air.

"You look so fucking good like this," Maeve whispered, leaning in, letting her breath graze Lolo's temple. "Wearing nothing but my shirt. Kneeling. Ruined."

Lolo let out a broken cry.

"You're going to come just like this," Maeve murmured. "No teasing. No games. Just because I want to watch you fall apart."

She pressed her palm harder. Lolo's thighs trembled. Her body arched, hands gripping Maeve's calf now for balance, her moans higher, sharper.

## Chapter 5: Respawn

"Say it," Maeve said. "Say who owns you."

"You do," Lolo sobbed. "Fuck—Maeve—please, please, I can't—"

"You can," Maeve growled. "You will."

Lolo came with a strangled, feral cry—her body shaking, eyes squeezed shut, back bowed. Maeve didn't stop. She held her there, grinding slowly through the aftershocks until Lolo slumped forward, boneless and slick with sweat.

Maeve eased her fingers free and gently cupped Lolo's cheek.

They stayed like that—Maeve sitting tall, Lolo crumpled against her, gasping, blissed-out and trembling. The flannel was soaked. Her skin glowed.

Finally, Lolo looked up. Her lips were swollen, her eyes dazed, but her grin was unmistakable.

"Next time," she panted, "I'm waking you up with the Switch in one hand… and your strap in the other."

Maeve smirked. "Only if you're ready for round two."

Maeve let out a low, wicked laugh. "Keep talking like that, and you'll never get breakfast again."

Lolo smirked. "Worth it."

Maeve tugged her back onto the bed and kissed her like the sun hadn't risen yet. Like nothing else needed building but this.

# Chapter 6: Kitchen Quiet, Streaming Loud

Maeve didn't think of herself as the jealous type. She didn't throw things, didn't accuse, didn't spiral into hypotheticals. She built. She repaired. She adjusted to what needed reinforcement. So when the flickers of possessiveness started showing up, tight across her shoulders and burning at the base of her throat like the edge of an insult she didn't say out loud, she ignored it. Or tried to.

It started small. A look Lolo gave the camera. A laugh that lingered too long. The way she said someone's username—sweet, soft, like she meant it.

Maeve was in the kitchen that night, barefoot, sleepless, her favorite mug in hand, stirring honey into black coffee while Lolo's voice poured in from the living room like ambient heat. The loft lights were low. The air was quiet but charged, that storm-still feeling after too many days of emotional tension gone unspoken.

Lolo was midstream. Her setup glowed warm and soft, the camera angled just right to catch her in thigh-highs and one of Maeve's old construction tees, knotted at the waist. She looked like chaos tucked into comfort, hair up, lip gloss on, eyeliner winged like sin. She played Dreamlight Valley with deliberate ease, her fingers dancing across the controller like everything she touched should want to be held by her.

The chat was active—too active.

Maeve sipped her coffee, forcing herself not to glance at the monitor screen in the reflection of the oven door. She didn't need to see the username. She didn't want to hear it again.

"Oh," Lolo said brightly. "Hammer_hottie, thank you for the sub! You've been so generous lately. I hope you know it means the world." A pause. Then: "You're sweet enough to build something with me."

The cabinet slammed.

Not intentionally. Not consciously. But it happened all the same—wood hitting wood with a force that echoed into the quiet. The spoon in Maeve's mug clinked too loudly. She reached for the bread on autopilot, her fingers trembling just enough to make the slices uneven. Butter smeared too thick. The pan hissed when it met the heat.

## Chapter 6: Kitchen Quiet, Streaming Loud

In the other room, Lolo hesitated.

Only for a moment. But Maeve heard it. The slight hitch in her voice. The way her smile softened, like paint cracking under pressure. She recovered instantly. Laughed. Read the next comment. Played through the discomfort like a pro. Like someone used to performing through friction.

Maeve didn't speak.

Lolo ended the stream fifteen minutes later. She closed the laptop softly, muted the mic with practiced grace, and walked into the kitchen with that same deliberate calm that always preceded something dangerous.

"You good?" she asked.

Maeve didn't turn around. She flipped the grilled cheese with surgical precision. "Fine."

"That cabinet sounded like it owed you money."

"Maybe it did."

Lolo leaned against the counter, arms crossed, bare legs brushing the cabinet door. "You gonna tell me what's actually going on, or do I get to guess?"

Maeve finally turned. Her eyes were sharp, but not cruel. "You thanked someone for building something with you."

Lolo blinked, then laughed—short, dry, surprised. "It's a stream joke, Maeve."

"You think I don't know what flirtation looks like?"

"I think you don't know what streaming is."

Maeve's jaw tightened. "It felt personal."

Lolo didn't flinch. "It wasn't."

"It sounded like it was."

Lolo stepped closer, tone cooling. "You jealous of chat now?"

Maeve didn't answer.

Lolo tilted her head. "Do you think what happens on that screen means more than what happens in this loft?"

"I think," Maeve said slowly, "that sometimes it feels like I'm sharing you. And I didn't sign up for that."

That landed. Not just between them, but inside Lolo—her posture shifted, her weight adjusted. She reached up, tugged the band from her hair, letting her curls fall wild around her shoulders.

"You think I'm giving parts of myself away for free?" she asked, quieter now.

## Chapter 6: Kitchen Quiet, Streaming Loud

Maeve didn't reply.

"Because I can promise you," Lolo said, stepping forward again, voice steadier, darker, "none of them get this. They don't get the flannel. They don't get the bruises. They don't get to see me come undone in your hands, or cook eggs in your kitchen, or fight about cabinet doors."

Maeve stared at her. "You're good at making people feel like they matter."

"It's literally my job."

"That's the problem."

"No, Maeve," Lolo snapped, and this time her voice cracked— not with anger, but with something more raw. "The problem is you don't know how to trust that I'm not performing with you. That you might actually matter more."

Maeve's breath caught. Not because she was hurt, but because it was true.

Lolo wasn't asking to be chased. She wasn't asking for apologies. She was asking for belief. For something steady. For someone who wouldn't see her light and flinch like it burned too hot.

Maeve set down the spatula and walked forward.

She stood in front of her with hands that didn't reach out, but itched to. "I don't know how to do this," she admitted. "Not like you do."

Lolo stepped in. Rested her forehead against Maeve's. "I don't need you to perform. I just need you to stay."

Maeve's hand found her hip. Gentle now. Grounded. "Even when I'm terrible at it?"

"Especially then."

They didn't kiss. Not right away. They just breathed. Close. Unmoving. The grilled cheese burned. Neither of them noticed.

Eventually, Maeve leaned back, opened the fridge, pulled out two ciders, and handed one over.

"You're ridiculous," she said.

"You're feral," Lolo replied.

They stood in the kitchen, shoulder to shoulder, sipping slowly, with the heat between them simmered low.Not extinguished. Just reined in.

For now.

# Chapter 7: Load-Bearing Tension

There were rules on a construction site. Lines drawn in dust and concrete—some legal, some unwritten. Maeve followed all of them. But nowhere in the manual did it say what to do when the woman you were seeing showed up in a silk blouse and velvet heels and started flirting with your second-in-command just to make you watch.

Lolo wasn't subtle. That had never been her brand. She perched on a half-assembled railing like a cat on a windowsill, legs crossed, smile sweet and sharp as a nail gun. Her voice rose a touch too bright when she called out to Eli, Maeve's longest-standing crew lead, about the lighting fixture height. She tilted her head, let a curl fall perfectly into her eyes, and smiled in that way that meant nothing—and everything.

Maeve stood ten feet away, drywall smudged on her forearm, clipboard forgotten. She didn't speak. She didn't move. But something behind her eyes darkened.

Eli answered politely—professionally, even—but the damage was done. Lolo wasn't trying to seduce anyone. She was trying to provoke.

It worked.

The rest of the day passed in taut, uneasy silence. Lolo didn't approach Maeve. Didn't need to. The look Maeve gave her once—a flick of the eyes, a clench of the jaw—was enough to pull something tight in Lolo's belly and make her sit a little straighter for the rest of the afternoon.

Maeve didn't address it until hours later.

The site was quiet. Crew gone. Only the echo of wind and distant traffic vibrated against the scaffolding. Maeve locked the main entrance behind them without a word. Lolo followed her up the unfinished stairwell to the second floor—now just a frame of future rooms, exposed beams, dangling wires, and silence.

There was a full-length mirror leaning against a support column, leftover from a staging mock-up. Maeve stopped in front of it. Turned. Looked at Lolo.

"Strip," Maeve said.

Lolo's smile faltered—just a beat, just a breath—but she obeyed.

She always did, eventually.

## Chapter 7: Load-Bearing Tension

The black silk blouse came first, her fingers moving slowly, unbuttoning one at a time like she knew she was being studied. Each inch of revealed skin felt hotter in the cool unfinished space. Her bra was sheer, barely there, the dark peaks of her nipples already hard. Maeve said nothing—just watched, heat simmering low in her gut.

Then came the skirt. Tight, wine-colored, hugging the curve of Lolo's hips like it had been poured on. She shimmied it down with practiced grace, revealing thigh-high stockings with lace tops and a pair of barely-there panties. Her heels made a soft, decisive click as they landed on the concrete. When she was down to nothing but lingerie and defiance, she stood tall, spine straight, chin tilted.

"What did I do this time?" she asked, eyes sharp even as her breath caught.

Maeve didn't answer. She stepped forward slowly, pulling a length of deep burgundy velvet ribbon from her back pocket. The color matched the flush starting to bloom across Lolo's chest.

Lolo raised her arms, wrists crossed.

Maeve bound her without a word. Every knot was deliberate. Every loop was a lesson. The ribbon wound around her wrists, snug but never cruel, and then Maeve tied the ends to a rafter beside the mirror—high enough to pull her body open, to bare her entirely.

## Nail Me Down

When she stepped back, Lolo's chest rose and fell in shallow, shaky breaths.

Maeve took in the sight of her—nipples peaked, stomach tensed, the muscles in her thighs visibly trembling from anticipation and restraint.

"You're mad," Lolo whispered.

Maeve stepped in close, pressing her body against Lolo's back. Her voice was low, dangerous. "I'm focused. And I'm going to teach you something."

She moved behind her, lips grazing Lolo's ear. "You like pushing my limits. Like making me watch you flirt with my second-in-command like it's a fucking game."

Lolo trembled. "I like when you snap."

Maeve's hand slid down her side and cupped her ass, squeezing hard enough to make Lolo gasp. "That wasn't flirting, was it?"

"No," Lolo panted.

"Then what was it?"

Lolo's breath hitched. "A test."

Maeve's hand cracked against her ass—loud, sharp, enough to echo off steel beams. Lolo jerked in the restraints, her body jerking forward, a whimper slipping free.

## Chapter 7: Load-Bearing Tension

Maeve slapped her again. "You passed," she growled.

Then she dropped to her knees and dragged her tongue across the red imprint blooming on Lolo's skin, the mark already rising. Lolo shivered violently.

Maeve didn't waste time. She slipped one hand between Lolo's trembling thighs and moaned softly when she found slickness waiting. "Of course you're soaked. Fucking mess."

She stood, grabbed Lolo by the hair, and forced her to look into the mirror. "You see that?" she said, voice pure grit. "That's what you look like when you're begging to be ruined."

Lolo whimpered, face flushed, eyes locked on her reflection.

Maeve edged her slowly. One hand between her thighs, fingers slicking lazy, cruel circles around her clit. The other gripping her hip, keeping her right where she wanted her. "Watch. Every second. You don't get to look away."

Lolo tried to close her eyes—Maeve slapped her thigh. "Open."

Maeve teased, then retreated. Again. And again. Lolo's hips bucked forward. Her voice rose in helpless gasps. Maeve growled filth into her ear the whole time.

"Look at yourself. Look how fucking pathetic you are. Begging. Drooling. Your thighs shaking from how badly you want it."

"Please," Lolo sobbed. "Please, please—"

## Nail Me Down

Maeve slipped two fingers in fast, no warning.

Lolo cried out, loud, wrecked, her body jolting forward.

Maeve didn't stop. She curled her fingers and pumped, slow and punishing, her thumb grinding over Lolo's clit in tight, merciless circles.

"This body was built for ruin," Maeve growled into her neck. "And I'm the one holding the fucking hammer."

Lolo shattered.

Her orgasm ripped through her like a scream made flesh—knees buckling, hands clenched in velvet, mouth open and soundless until the moan broke free. Maeve held her in place, fucked her through it, fingers relentless.

"Don't you dare stop coming," she hissed. "I'm not finished with you."

Lolo sobbed again. Her thighs slick. Her breath gone. Her voice nothing but moans and gratitude and need.

When she finally slumped in her bonds, trembling and wet and marked, Maeve untied her with slow, steady fingers and caught her just before she fell.

She carried her to a patch of drop cloths in the corner, like she weighed nothing, sat with her on the floor, holding her against her chest.

## Chapter 7: Load-Bearing Tension

Lolo clung to her, eyes glassy, lashes wet with mascara streaks.

"I hate you a little," she whispered, voice wrecked.

Maeve kissed her temple. "No, you don't."

Lolo laughed—a broken, grateful sound—and buried her face in Maeve's neck. "You're right."

Outside, the city groaned under its weight.

Inside, Maeve kissed her again. And Lolo finally let herself be still.

Inside, Maeve's arms were scaffolding. And Lolo? Lolo had never felt safer inside her own wreckage.

# Chapter 8: Ghosts Don't Bring Flowers

The flowers arrived without warning, sleek and smug in their black box with gold-embossed script. They looked like something that belonged in a luxury showroom—not a construction site caked in dust and splintered expectation. Six perfect white roses, glossy and sharp-edged as bone. Too elegant. Too cold. Lolo's name was printed across the envelope in looping, expensive strokes.

Maeve hadn't seen them delivered. She came back from a midday supply run to find them sitting on her work table—dead center like a warning flare. The crew had cleared out early for an HVAC delay, and Lolo stood alone near the roll away tool rack, arms folded over her chest, mouth tight.

Maeve froze at the threshold. Her eyes didn't leave the box.

## Chapter 8: Ghosts Don't Bring Flowers

"From him?" she asked.

Lolo's voice was quiet. Flat. "Yeah."

Maeve said nothing.

There were a hundred ways she could've responded. She could've asked how he got this address. She could've demanded to know how often he reached out. She could've raged, stormed, made Lolo feel like a threat instead of a person. But Maeve Kincaid didn't explode. She built.

She walked to the table, lifted the box by one corner, and without a word, carried it across the room and dropped it into the industrial trash bin. The sound was small, final. She didn't flinch.

Lolo didn't move. She didn't look surprised. She looked tired.

The rest of the day unraveled in silence. No taunts, no tension. Just two women walking the perimeter of something too sharp to name. Maeve took measurements she didn't need to recheck. Lolo stared at the client's lighting plan like it had personally offended her. Neither of them acknowledged what had just happened. There were no fights. No apologies.

That night, Maeve didn't touch her.

She made tea. Set it next to the couch where Lolo curled under a blanket with her headset on. The stream played quietly in the background—an older one. No camera. Just her voice, soft and steady, narrating a digital harvest. She didn't go live that night. She didn't say why.

Maeve kept glancing over from her workbench, watching her in profile. Lolo looked small like that, bundled and hunched, her usual chaos dimmed into something almost delicate. Maeve wanted to say something. She didn't. Her silence wasn't cruel. It was careful.

She waited until Lolo went to bed.

Then she got to work.

The drawer had been there for months—an unfinished slot beneath Maeve's side of the bedframe, originally intended for spare batteries and odds and ends she never bothered to store. She pulled it from the base and laid it across her worktable, sanding the raw wood until it gleamed. The grain was rough, but it had character—like scars that didn't need covering.

Maeve didn't sketch blueprints. She didn't need to. Her body already knew the measurements by heart.

She lined the inside with midnight velvet, scavenged from an old photography backdrop Lolo had tossed into the donate pile a month ago. It had smelled like her even then. She cut the lining with precision, secured it with wood glue and clamps, then reached into her stash. A pair of soft restraints. A roll of silk. The red lace bralette she'd torn in haste, still tucked in the corner of the laundry drawer. She placed each item inside with the care of someone curating history.

## Chapter 8: Ghosts Don't Bring Flowers

There were no locks. No labels.

Just space. Just invitation.

She slid the drawer back into place before the sun rose and got into bed without waking Lolo. Her hands smelled like sawdust. Her shoulders ached. She slept like someone who had finally made room.

The next day passed with quiet, gentle normalcy. Lolo didn't mention the flowers. Maeve didn't bring up the drawer.

Not until after dinner, when Maeve was at the sink, sleeves rolled, washing out a pan. Lolo wandered into the bedroom looking for her phone charger. She opened the nightstand by instinct.

She froze.

She didn't say anything right away.

Maeve heard the drawer click closed. Heard footsteps—slower now. Not hesitant. Just heavier.

Lolo returned to the kitchen, bare feet silent against the floor, and perched herself on the counter like she had a hundred times before. Only this time, she didn't speak. She just watched Maeve rinse the sponge, set the pan aside, and dry her hands on a cloth.

Then she said, "You made me a drawer."

Maeve didn't look up. "You needed somewhere to put your things."

"It's lined in velvet."

"It's what I had."

Lolo swallowed. "That was your photography cloth."

Maeve nodded. "It wasn't doing much in storage."

Silence stretched between them again, but not tense this time. Not painful. Just thick with everything neither of them had words for.

Then, softly, "You love in sawdust and screws, don't you?"

Maeve finally looked at her.

Her voice was low when she said, "I love in what lasts."

Lolo's chest rose slowly, her eyes unreadable.

Then she slid off the counter and crossed the room in three steps.

She didn't touch Maeve. She didn't kiss her. She just pressed her forehead to Maeve's, breath uneven, hands trembling faintly at her sides.

"You didn't ask who he was," she whispered.

## Chapter 8: Ghosts Don't Bring Flowers

"I didn't want to know."

"I would've told you."

"I didn't need it."

Lolo pulled back, just enough to meet her eyes. "Why?"

"Because ghosts don't bring flowers," Maeve said. "They just haunt things. I build them."

It wasn't poetry. It was fact.

It gutted Lolo.

She wrapped her arms around Maeve's waist and held on tightly, her cheek resting over Maeve's heart. They stood like that until the kitchen lights buzzed and the outside world faded.

Later that night, when Lolo reached for her in bed, she didn't demand. She didn't tease. She just whispered, "Let me stay."

Maeve pulled her close and didn't let go.

## Chapter 9: Pixel Kinks

The streaming overlay was pink and silver, all gothic filigree and hand-coded sparkle. Lolo had commissioned it from a mutual she trusted—someone who knew how to make a Twitch layout feel like a boudoir and a battlefield at once. The frame around her webcam shimmered like old velvet. Her chatroom glowed with custom emotes: bats, roses, tiny flannels, a cursed emoji of Maeve's scowling face. The banner read, 'Live from the loft. Cozy chaos, controlled burns only'.

It was Saturday night. Rain on the window, rosemary in the diffuser, and a half-eaten quesadilla on the desk. Lolo sat in her gaming chair, headset snug, black silk robe tied loose over an old tour tee that wasn't hers. Her thighs gleamed, bare from mid-hip to calf, and she'd skipped pants entirely—though no one on stream would ever know. Her face was lit just enough to cast drama on her cheekbones and mischief in her smile.

## Chapter 9: Pixel Kinks

She was playing Dreamlight again, slow and indulgent. Farming pumpkins. Rearranging decor. Her avatar, a chaos witch version of herself, had just placed a demonic-looking bookshelf next to the castle fountain when the stream began to find its rhythm.

Maeve had been behind her for the last half-hour, off-camera, pretending to scroll through news on her phone from the couch, but Lolo could feel her watching. Not just idly. With the kind of attention that made the back of her neck heat. Not possessive, exactly. But present. Solid.

Lolo shifted in her chair and said, too brightly, "This one's for the flannel fiends in chat. You know who you are."

The emotes exploded.

Behind her, Maeve didn't move.

So Lolo decided to push.

It started small. Subtle and almost innocent. A slow lean back into her chair, hips tilting just enough to arch her lower back invitingly. Her voice dipped half an octave, syrupy and suggestive as she murmured into the mic, "Mmm, that placement's perfect. Just a little to the left, and—yeah, right there."

The chat reacted immediately—flooding with emotes, hearts, jokes she pretended not to see.

She smiled, a slow, wicked thing. "You're all so filthy tonight," she purred, smoothing her hands down her thighs. "Should I be worried?"

Still no sound from behind her.

But Lolo could feel Maeve's stare—the weight of it like a physical thing dragging across her skin. She could feel the tension winding tighter by the second. She smirked, setting her controller casually on her lap, and rose midstream—camera still carefully framed from the ribs up—walking off-screen with a sway to her hips that was absolutely on purpose.

She returned seconds later carrying her Switch and a grin sharp enough to draw blood.

Maeve was sprawled on the couch—broad shoulders, heavy gaze, one arm over the back like a throne. Unreadable. Dangerous.

Lolo didn't ask.

She climbed into Maeve's lap, straddling her boldly, one knee on either side, silk robe falling open just enough to tease the camera. She let out a little sigh, all mock-innocent. "My chair's killing my back. Hope you don't mind."

Maeve didn't answer.

Didn't need to.

## Chapter 9: Pixel Kinks

Lolo powered on the Switch again, shifted her weight deliberately so that her ass pressed firmly against Maeve's thighs, and started playing. On camera, all viewers saw was a slightly closer angle of her face and a suspicious change in breathing.

"Let's move some boulders, babes," she murmured into the mic, fingers dancing lightly over the controls as she rocked her hips in tiny, rolling movements.

Maeve's hand landed on her waist, firm. Final. A warning.

Lolo smiled sweetly and kept grinding.

She leaned back just enough to whisper, only for Maeve: "You're so tense, babe. Maybe you need to let go."

Maeve's voice rasped against her ear, low and cutting. "Do not make me pause your game."

The threat sent a shiver down Lolo's spine.

But she couldn't help herself.

Maeve's fingers slipped under the edge of her robe, dragging slow up her bare inner thigh. Teasing. Threatening.

Lolo barely managed to click her character forward on screen, forcing a laugh into her voice. "Gonna move that rock—oof, that's a big one—ah, so hard to handle."

The chat went feral.

*Nail Me Down*

Maeve's fingers moved higher.

Lolo shifted forward, trying not to squirm openly, but her breathing had gone ragged.

"You're trying to distract me," Maeve murmured, her hand resting maddeningly close to the heat between Lolo's legs.

"You distracted me first," Lolo whispered back, cheeks flushed.

"You're streaming."

"You're touching me while I'm streaming."

"You're grinding on my lap in my clothes. With nothing fucking underneath."

"Is it working?"

Maeve slipped two fingers beneath the robe, found her soaked, and dragged a slow, brutal stroke along Lolo's slit.

Lolo gasped audibly, scrambling to mute the mic with a shaky tap.

"Say it," Maeve growled, fingers circling lightly, not giving her enough pressure to satisfy. "Say what you want."

Lolo whimpered, clutching the Switch uselessly. Her avatar stood frozen on screen beside a pond, little pixelated sparkles twinkling while the chat begged for movement.

## Chapter 9: Pixel Kinks

Maeve edged her mercilessly—fingers teasing just shy of her clit, never quite giving her what she needed. Lolo's hips rocked helplessly against her thigh.

"Please," she finally moaned, voice cracked and desperate. "I want to come."

Maeve's breath was hot against her ear. "You muted?"

"I think so," Lolo panted.

"Better be sure."

Lolo whimpered, fumbling to unmute, clearing her throat theatrically into the mic. "Sorry, guys—had to yell at Maeve for unplugging the extension cord again. We're back."

Maeve's fingers slammed deep inside her at the exact moment the words left her mouth.

Lolo nearly dropped the console.

She muted the mic again with a strangled gasp.

"Fuck—Maeve—please, I need—" she sobbed.

Maeve pressed her thumb cruelly against her clit, grinding slow circles just light enough to deny.

"Say it," Maeve said again, that low growl that undid her.

## Nail Me Down

"Let me come," Lolo begged, rocking her hips hard against Maeve's hand. "Please, Daddy, please—"

Maeve kissed her ear. "Good girl."

Then she let her.

Lolo came hard, biting down on her fist to muffle her scream, her body convulsing on Maeve's lap. The game still played quietly in the background—a fish splashed in the digital pond, oblivious to the wreckage unfolding behind the screen.

Maeve held her steady, fucking her through it with slow, ruthless precision until Lolo sagged boneless against her, robe open, legs twitching from the overstimulation.

When she finally went limp, forehead pressed against Maeve's shoulder, still panting, she whispered, "I hate you."

Maeve chuckled low in her throat, wrapping the robe tighter around her trembling form, dropping a kiss against her sweat-damp temple.

"You better not mute me next time," Lolo whispered, voice wrecked but smiling.

"Then don't test me on camera," Maeve murmured back.

Lolo grinned, legs still trembling, heart still hammering against Maeve's chest. "It's literally my brand."

## Chapter 9: Pixel Kinks

Maeve kissed her again, deep and slow.

This time—just this time—she let her win.

## Chapter 10: Fallout

It started like most of their fights: offhand, offbeat, and not as important as it felt in the moment. Lolo was midstream, curled in her gaming chair, camera angled perfectly, hair pinned up with black ribbon and gloss still intact. The chat was lively. Emotes filled the screen. Someone had just donated a ridiculous amount to unlock new overlay animations. Lolo clapped, laughed, and said something flirty, maybe too flirty—something like "You're all just here for the thighs and threats, don't lie."

Maeve had been sitting on the edge of the bed, watching. Not actively. Just in her periphery. Working on site renderings. Answering client emails. Trying not to let the growing coil of frustration in her chest tighten too far. It wasn't about the chat. Not really. It was the way Lolo talked when the mic was on. The way she smiled—bright, hungry, performative. Maeve loved that smile. But not when it felt like a mask she didn't get to keep.

## Chapter 10: Fallout

Lolo said something else then, to a repeat subscriber, something playful: "You always bring the best energy. Maybe I should add you to my dungeon build."

Maeve looked up.

"That's enough," she said. Quiet. Clipped.

Lolo didn't hear. Or she didn't register the tone.

Maeve stood, crossed the room, and leaned just off camera.

"Maeve?" Lolo asked, turning slightly.

"I said that's enough."

The smile faded. "Babe, I'm just—"

Maeve's jaw tightened. "You don't stop, do you? You don't know how."

Lolo blinked. "It's a joke. It's my stream."

"It's not just your stream," Maeve said. "It's our fucking life."

The mic was still hot.

The chat went still.

Maeve didn't realize it. Lolo did. Too late.

"Not now," Lolo hissed, eyes wide. She reached to mute—fumbled.

"You're too much," Maeve said, and her voice cracked on the words. Not loud. But final.

Silence.

Lolo stared at her. Pale. Mouth open, breathing too fast.

And then she stood.

Without muting. Without explanation.

She left her headset on the chair and walked out of frame, out of the room, out of the loft.

The door didn't slam. That almost made it worse.

The chat lit up like a bomb. Emojis. Questions. Panic. Someone clipped the moment. Someone else tweeted it.

Maeve stood in the middle of the room, blinking.

The air was thick with the echo of what she'd just said, and what she didn't mean. Or maybe did. In the moment. That was the worst part. It had come from somewhere.

But now it was out there. Lolo was gone.

She walked to the computer, stared at the open stream window,

## Chapter 10: Fallout

the scrolling chaos of concerned usernames and speculative text.

She clicked the feed off.

The screen went black.

She didn't cry.

She didn't call after her.

She picked up the headset and set it down neatly. Then she grabbed her tool belt.

There was nothing left to say. Only something to build.

By the time she reached the rooftop, the wind had picked up. It wasn't cold—not yet—but the air had that edge, the kind that made her feel awake in the wrong ways. She looked around the bare flat expanse of the building, her boots scuffing against gravel and old cigarette burns. She remembered Lolo pointing up at the sky a month ago, offhandedly, and saying, "This would be a perfect place for lavender."

Maeve started clearing debris.

It was slow work. Tedious. Physical. Perfect.

She worked by headlamp light and the glow of her phone screen. She hauled planks up the stairwell alone, built raised planter beds from pressure-treated wood she'd intended for an unused client deck. She filled them with soil from bags she kept in the supply closet—intended for weight balancing, not beauty.

It didn't matter.

What mattered was movement.

What mattered was making something.

She didn't eat. Didn't stop. Her fingers split. Her muscles burned. She didn't care.

By the time she installed the blackout curtain railings—industrial, leftover from a failed theater renovation—it was past midnight.

She hung the curtains on wire hooks, thick navy velvet from old studio props. She screwed in LED lights along the baseboard, warm yellow. She arranged six lavender plants she'd salvaged from a nursery into a half-moon shape around a bench she'd built on the spot. Simple. Sturdy. Hers.

The bench creaked when she sat. She looked out over the city skyline, still dotted with windows and blinking lights, and let her hands fall to her knees.

She didn't feel victorious.

She felt raw.

Lolo had been right. She didn't know how to speak. Not when

## Chapter 10: Fallout

it counted.

Maeve could praise with her hands. Command with her body. Wreck with purpose. But words? Words turned sharp when she got scared. And Lolo—Lolo had never been small. Never been something you could box in or brace against. She spilled over. She demanded space.

Maeve had loved her for that.

Right up until she used it as an excuse to push her away.

She sat there until the lights flickered. Until the smell of lavender filled her lungs. Until the wind softened and her shoulders stopped shaking.

Maeve stared at what she'd made.

It wasn't an apology.

But it was a beginning. Something to express what she couldn't say.

I hurt you.

I miss you.

This is for you. Come back when you're ready.

If you don't, at least I built something that will last. Just like I promised.

# Chapter 11: Patch Notes

Lolo didn't knock when she returned.

She didn't want to announce herself. Not because she was angry—though part of her still was—but because the act of knocking implied she was a guest. A stranger, which she wasn't. Not here. Not after everything. Not after nights wrapped in flannel and breathless declarations made with hands instead of mouths. Not after being built into the bones of this place.

The loft was silent.

She stepped inside with her keys still clutched between her knuckles. The lamp in the far corner was on, casting a soft amber pool across the concrete floor. Maeve was sitting at the workbench, elbows on her knees, back slightly hunched like someone who hadn't moved in hours.

## Chapter 11: Patch Notes

Lolo didn't speak.

Maeve looked up. Her face was unreadable. Not closed. Just tired in a way that felt too familiar.

"I want to show you something," Maeve said.

No explanation. No apology.

Lolo hesitated, but she nodded. Not because she was ready. But because some part of her still wanted to understand.

They didn't speak as they moved. The stairwell was quiet, each step a marker between before and after. When Maeve opened the rooftop door, the scent hit first—earth, wood, and lavender heavy in the night air. The blackout curtains were drawn half-open, framing the rooftop like a stage or a sanctuary. Light from hidden LED strips glowed along the base of raised beds and stone tiles, casting the space in gold.

Lolo stopped walking.

She didn't gasp. She didn't cry. She just stood there, wind in her curls, watching the garden breathe.

Lavender, six plants in full bloom. A low bench, hand-carved. A velvet curtain that blocked the city lights. A quiet place made with the kind of care that only came from knowing someone down to their bones.

Maeve didn't say anything for a long time. Then finally, she spoke—her voice quiet and rough.

"I can't say what I mean. Not always. But I built this for staying."

Lolo turned slowly.

Maeve wasn't trying to explain. Or justify. She was just standing there, hands at her sides, shoulders loose in surrender.

"This is how I speak," Maeve said. "Wood. Nails. Things that don't get deleted when I screw up."

"You called me too much," Lolo said.

It wasn't an accusation. It was just the truth. A wound recited from memory.

Maeve flinched.

"I was scared," she admitted. "That I wouldn't be enough. That you'd outpace me. That I'd try and fail, and you'd still be smiling for someone else's camera."

"That wasn't yours to say," Lolo replied. "And not like that."

Maeve nodded. "I know."

They stood with the whole garden between them. Wind in the curtains. Lavender brushing against cedar.

"I thought about how to apologize," Maeve said. "And then I

## Chapter 11: Patch Notes

realized I don't have the right words. I never have. But I can make things. I can hold them steady. And I can stay."

Lolo crossed the distance.

She didn't speak.

She didn't kiss her.

She just sat down on the stone floor beside the bench. Quiet. Deliberate.

Maeve followed and sat beside her. Knees touching.

They stayed that way for a long time. No movement. No questions. Just air. Just breath.

Lolo's voice broke the stillness first. "You scare me."

Maeve's throat tightened. "Because I hurt you?"

"Because you don't say anything until it's already broken."

Maeve didn't look away. "I'm trying to learn."

"You don't have to be perfect," Lolo whispered. "But you can't stay silent and expect me to guess."

Maeve closed her eyes. "I won't ask you to."

Another pause.

"I didn't know if you'd come back," Maeve said.

"I didn't either," Lolo replied.

They didn't speak for a while after that. They didn't have to. Lolo reached out and threaded her fingers with Maeve's, palm to palm. They sat like that, watching the lavender sway.

"I've never had someone build something for me," Lolo said eventually.

Maeve glanced over. "You're worth building for."

Tears stung at the edge of Lolo's eyes. She blinked them away. "I don't forgive you. Not yet."

"I don't expect you to."

"But I'm still here."

Maeve nodded. "So am I."

And maybe that was the only patch note they needed tonight.

Not a fix. Not a full update.

Just still here. Still trying. Still them.

They stayed until the wind changed.

Until Lolo's head found Maeve's shoulder.

## Chapter 11: Patch Notes

Until the garden, born out of guilt, became something more: a shared space. A blueprint for healing.

The soft, unsaid promise beneath all of it.

I'll stay. As long as you let me.

## Chapter 12: Velvet Leash

⁓⊙⃝⊙⁓

It started with a joke. At least, Lolo meant it that way.

They were out—first time in weeks. A friend-of-a-friend's housewarming party in a glassy apartment stacked high above the city. Everyone was dressed in casual flex: messy eyeliner, clean boots, a denim jacket that probably cost three hundred dollars. Lolo fit in perfectly. Maeve didn't. Not really. But she stood beside Lolo with her sleeves rolled to the elbows and her stare set to neutral. Holding her drink. Holding her ground.

Someone had said something—something stupid about Lolo's stream numbers and her "marketing genius." Lolo had smiled, too sharp, too sweet, and curled her hand possessively around Maeve's forearm.

"What can I say?" she said, voice smooth. "Daddy funds the operation."

## Chapter 12: Velvet Leash

Maeve didn't flinch. Didn't blink.

But the glass in her hand creaked.

Lolo didn't look at her.

She just smiled wider kept talking. As if the word hadn't detonated between them like a grenade laced with velvet.

Maeve didn't say anything all the way home. Not in the car. Not in the elevator. Not when she opened the door and waited for Lolo to walk in first.

Lolo toed off her boots and dropped her bag on the floor with a laugh that didn't quite land.

"You okay?" she asked, already pulling off her jacket.

Maeve shut the door behind them. Locked it.

Then turned around.

Her voice was calm. Controlled. Maeve's voice was level. Cold steel wrapped in velvet.

"Say it again."

Lolo blinked, heart leaping. "What?"

Maeve didn't raise her voice. Didn't need to.

"In the kitchen. Now."

There was no room for play in her tone. Just promise.

Lolo's skin prickled. She moved.

Barefoot, body humming with tension, she crossed the loft's floor with the sway of someone who knew what was coming and craved it. The weight of Maeve's stare followed her—heat pressed between her shoulder blades like a hand not yet touching.

By the time she reached the island, she didn't have to turn around to know Maeve was behind her.

So close. Still not touching.

The kitchen was quiet, save for the faint hum of the fridge. The under-cabinet lighting cast a warm glow over the countertop, but the rest of the room was in shadow. Lolo set her hands on the stone. Waited.

Maeve stepped in, placed her palm at the small of Lolo's back, and bent her forward.

Slow.

Deliberate.

Lolo's breath stuttered.

## *Chapter 12: Velvet Leash*

The stone was cold beneath her cheek. Her nipples tightened. Her core clenched with anticipation. She didn't resist. Didn't speak. She spread her legs wider and waited to be taken apart.

Maeve leaned in close, her voice a growl in her ear. "Say it again."

Lolo swallowed hard, the air thick and charged. "Daddy."

The first slap landed sharp and hot across her ass, echoing off the tile. Then another. Lolo cried out, jolted, hips bucking forward as pain bloomed into heat.

"Say it like you mean it," Maeve snapped.

"Daddy," Lolo moaned, louder this time, voice shaking.

Maeve grunted in approval.

She reached down and flipped up Lolo's skirt, exposing her bare ass. Maeve had torn the panties earlier in the week. Lolo hadn't replaced them.

"Fucking brat," Maeve muttered, dragging her callused fingers down the crease of Lolo's ass, across her soaked cunt. "You like putting on a show? Like calling me out in public? You think I won't answer you right then and there?"

Lolo whimpered, hips pressing back for more. "I wanted your attention."

## Nail Me Down

"You had all of it." Maeve grabbed her by the hips and yanked her back just enough to make her feel off-balance. "Now you'll learn what it costs to play games with me."

She reached into the drawer beside the fridge—the one with extra gloves, folded aprons, and the harness she kept there just in case. Just for this.

Maeve didn't tease. She didn't warn.

The sound of lube hitting skin, the rustle of leather being buckled on—it all filled the silence like thunder.

Then pressure.

Maeve lined up the cock and pushed in slow—but not gentle. Lolo gasped, her hands gripping the edge of the island as her body stretched, took it, welcomed it.

"Fuck," she moaned, high and broken.

Maeve didn't wait. She gripped Lolo's hip with one hand, the other tangled in her hair, and drove in deeper. Hard. Her thighs met the back of Lolo's ass with a smack. The sound of skin meeting skin was obscene and glorious.

"This pussy's mine," Maeve snarled into her ear. "You parade it around like it's not. Like I won't bend you over and use it wherever I fucking want."

Lolo couldn't respond—could only sob a moan and press her

## Chapter 12: Velvet Leash

face into her arms.

Maeve pulled back and slammed in again, harder. The whole island shifted.

"You gonna be a good girl now?" she growled.

Lolo nodded frantically, voice lost to breathless gasps.

"Say it," Maeve hissed.

"Yes—yes, Daddy—good girl, I'll be good—"

Maeve's hand slipped between her legs. Two fingers found Lolo's clit already swollen and slick. She rubbed in tight, fast circles, her thrusts never faltering.

"You don't get to be quiet now," she said, pinching Lolo's nipple through her blouse with her free hand. "You wanted to act out? Now you scream for me."

Lolo screamed.

Low and sharp. It echoed. It broke open in her throat.

Maeve kept fucking her—deep and brutal, but never careless. Her rhythm was perfect. Measured. Engineered to destroy.

Lolo trembled, thighs quaking, the counter damp with sweat, her own slick dripping down her inner thighs.

## Nail Me Down

"Who do you belong to?" Maeve barked, pounding harder.

"You!" Lolo gasped. "You—fuck, Daddy—please—"

"Say it again."

"You, Daddy. I belong to you."

Maeve growled low, pure feral pleasure.

"You get off on being used like this, don't you?"

"Yes—yes—I love it—please—don't stop—"

Maeve didn't.

She held Lolo down, fucked her through her first orgasm—watching her collapse forward, body locking up, legs jerking. Then kept going.

Until the second wave broke her.

Until she sobbed and shook and choked on her breath, her body going limp under the weight of it.

Only then did Maeve pull out, slowly, gently, setting the harness aside.

Lolo was wrecked—smeared with sweat and slick, skirt still hiked around her waist, flushed and radiant. Maeve caught her before her knees buckled, lifting her with ease and settling her

## Chapter 12: Velvet Leash

onto the counter like glassware she built herself.

She kissed Lolo slow and deep. Tongue tasting salt. Fingers brushing tears off her cheeks with the same hand that had held her down.

"You wanted to be claimed," Maeve murmured, voice hoarse.

Lolo nodded, eyes glassy. "I needed it."

Maeve smiled. Not soft. Not sweet.

But real.

Lolo, wrecked and glowing, whispered, "Finally."

# Chapter 13: Final Walkthrough

The brownstone was finished.

After months of deadlines and design meetings, supplier delays and late-night argument resolutions, it stood whole. Three floors of restored brick, custom hardwood, black iron railings, and velvet curtain trim stitched by hands that had bruised and cradled in equal measure. It had been gutted down to its bones and rebuilt. Better. Just like them.

Maeve unlocked the front door without fanfare. She didn't announce the walkthrough, didn't call out when she stepped inside. Lolo followed without needing the invitation. Her heels echoed on the tile—slow, intentional. The silence wasn't awkward. It was reverent.

The space still smelled like cedar and paint, but fainter now. It had settled into itself. So had they.

## Chapter 13: Final Walkthrough

Lolo walked beside her as Maeve checked final placements—light switches, trim alignment, the way the custom bannister ran smoothly beneath her palm. Everything was perfect. Everything worked. She should've felt proud. Instead, she felt something deeper. Quieter.

Lolo didn't speak as they moved through the kitchen, the living room, the sunlit corner nook where they'd first argued over insulation placement. She only looked. Occasionally smiled. Once, she ran her fingers over the edge of the butcher block island and said, "This feels like you."

Maeve didn't respond. She didn't need to.

The real moment came upstairs.

Lolo moved ahead of her on the final landing. She didn't pause at the top. She turned left, walked through the doorway of the master bedroom, and disappeared inside. Maeve followed, heartbeat steady but heavy.

The room was empty. No furniture. No lights yet. Just fresh white walls, sunlight pooling across dark floorboards, and Lolo standing in the center wearing black lace and nothing else.

Maeve stopped.

Lolo's hair was pinned up with precision. Her lips were painted dark, wine-red, and inviting. Her stockings shimmered in the golden light from the high windows, and she stood in the center of the empty room like she belonged there, like she'd been built for this exact space, for this exact moment. In her hand, she held a velvet leash. Deep red. The same shade as a bruise.

She didn't speak.

She simply offered it.

Maeve didn't ask questions. She didn't need to.

She crossed the room in steady, grounded steps and took the leash from her hand. Her thumb brushed over the smooth leather collar already circling Lolo's throat—unlocked, waiting. Maeve buckled it into place with slow, practiced fingers, the soft click sealing something that didn't need to be spoken aloud. She adjusted the leash between her fingers. Tugged once.

Lolo exhaled like she'd just let go of gravity.

They didn't speak.

Maeve began walking her backward. One step. Then another. The leash stayed taut between them, just enough to guide. Not yank. Just enough to say *you're mine.* Lolo followed silently, her dark eyes locked on Maeve's, her lips parted with breath she couldn't quite catch.

When her calves hit the edge of the low window bench, Maeve didn't stop.

She pressed her palm to Lolo's chest, firm, and pushed.

## Chapter 13: Final Walkthrough

Lolo sat.

Legs parted. Eyes wide. Breasts rising and falling in the lace bralette she hadn't bothered to cover. Her robe slid down her arms and pooled at her wrists. The collar looked obscene in so much light, so stark against her soft skin. Sacred.

Maeve dropped to her knees.

She kissed Lolo's inner thigh. Once. Then again. Tongue warm, breath humid. She let her mouth drag across skin like it was scripture.

Then she stood.

Wordless, she removed her belt. Unfastened the top button of her jeans. Stepped back long enough to strap into the harness she'd stashed in her toolbox two days ago—just in case Lolo made good on the promise in her eyes.

Lolo didn't move. Didn't breathe.

She just waited. Knees parted. Shoulders drawn back. Head slightly bowed.

Owned.

Maeve stepped between her thighs, curled her hand around the leash again, and gave it another tug. Not hard. Just enough to make Lolo look up at her, neck stretched, eyes shining.

## Nail Me Down

Maeve kissed her, slow and claiming. Then she took the leash in one hand and gently guided Lolo down to the polished floorboards. She rolled her onto her stomach, helped her up to her knees, then pushed her chest forward.

Face down. Ass up. Collar taut.

The leash trailed over Lolo's back like a ribbon, like the boundary between discipline and devotion. Maeve pushed the lace panties aside and spread her open, exposing her soaked cunt, her thighs already slick. She didn't tease. She didn't ask.

She lined up and pushed in.

Slow. But not gentle.

Lolo gasped—sharp and breathless—the sound of someone coming undone in one perfect, ruined exhale.

Maeve held her hips steady, letting her feel the stretch, the pressure, the way her body made space to take her. She paused there—deep, buried, possessive—and leaned forward, lips ghosting Lolo's ear.

"Feel that?" she whispered. "That's mine."

Then she started to move.

Her thrusts were slow at first, grounding. Then deeper. Harder. Her thighs slapped against Lolo's ass with every stroke, the leash slipping through her fingers with every pull.

## Chapter 13: Final Walkthrough

Lolo moaned—high, reedy, desperate. Her hands clenched into fists. Her body rocked back to meet each thrust like it hurt not to.

Maeve gripped her neck with one hand, the leash with the other.

"Who do you belong to?" she asked, voice low and guttural.

Lolo tried to answer, but it came out as a choked whimper.

Maeve fucked her harder.

The slap of skin against skin grew sharper. The floor creaked. The sound of Lolo's pleasure turned frantic.

"Say it."

"Y-you," Lolo gasped. "You—fuck, Daddy—I'm yours."

Maeve grabbed the leash, pulled her upright by the collar, and fucked her deep—one long, brutal stroke that had Lolo shaking against her.

"You are. Every fucking inch."

Lolo sobbed, nodding, her voice long gone.

Maeve leaned down, kissed her shoulder, and kept going.

She didn't stop until Lolo came—hard, clenching around her with a strangled cry, body buckling. Maeve held her through it, and then again when the second orgasm hit harder, longer, wrecking her completely.

Afterward, Maeve stayed kneeling behind her, her breathing heavy. Her hands roamed Lolo's back. Down her sides. She kissed the base of her spine. Traced the curve of her ass. Her thighs.

She unbuckled the collar slowly. Pressed her palm to Lolo's back like she was feeling for something under the skin. When she was sure Lolo could stand, she helped her roll onto her side, then her back.

She lifted her onto her lap and cradled her.

Lolo didn't speak. She didn't need to.

The collar was still around her neck. The leash draped across her bare chest. Her lips were swollen, her eyes glassy with the kind of bliss that couldn't be faked.

Maeve brushed the hair from her face. Let her fingers drift over every inch of marked, spent skin. Lolo pressed her cheek to Maeve's chest and sighed. The kind of sigh that meant safe.

They sat like that on the floor, surrounded by nothing but the sound of their breathing, the golden light, and the home they'd carved out of chaos.

Eventually, Lolo lifted her head, looked up, and pressed a kiss to Maeve's jaw.

*Chapter 13: Final Walkthrough*

"Let's stay," Maeve whispered, voice quiet and wrecked.

Lolo—still in her collar, still in Maeve's lap—nodded.

Because she already had.

## Chapter 14: Soft Reset

Maeve woke before the light reached the windows. It was a habit, rooted in years of job sites and sunrise briefings. But this morning, it felt different—not out of necessity, but reverence. She blinked slowly, breath quiet, and didn't move right away. Her eyes adjusted to the dark.

Lolo was wrapped around her.

The sheets were tangled low, barely clinging to her hips. Her leg draped over Maeve's thigh, her arm tucked beneath her pillow, hair a dark mess across both of them. It was the silk that Maeve noticed first—the soft gleam of it binding Lolo's wrists, knotted loose but deliberate, just as Maeve had tied them hours ago.

A choice. A ritual. A trust.

## Chapter 14: Soft Reset

Maeve let her eyes roam.

Lolo's body had always drawn her like blueprints—lines to study, curves to shape herself around. She was all hourglass and hunger, full thighs and soft belly, breasts rising and falling with each slow inhale. But this morning, it wasn't desire that rose first. It was awe.

Maeve moved carefully.

She pressed a kiss to Lolo's shoulder, then to the knot at her wrist. Her fingers traced over silk and skin, memorizing the warmth. Lolo stirred slightly, but didn't wake. Not yet.

Maeve shifted, her hand sliding low, palm grazing the curve of Lolo's belly. She loved this part of her—unapologetically full, soft in a way that made Maeve want to kneel. She dragged her thumb slowly along the seam of Lolo's inner thigh, then kissed her again, just under the breast. Lolo made a sound then, small and breathy, not quite conscious.

Maeve's voice was barely a whisper. "You're perfect when you sleep."

She kissed her again.

Then again.

Lower now.

Every touch was a prayer. A promise. Her lips moved along

Lolo's body with the kind of patience she rarely allowed herself, pressing into the swell of her stomach, the dip of her hip, the underside of her thigh. Maeve wanted to mark her. Not with teeth. Not with bruises. But with worship.

Lolo whimpered when Maeve's hand slipped between her legs.

Still tied. Still vulnerable.

Maeve's fingers stroked gently, barely there. She watched Lolo breathe through it, her hips twitching forward, still half-dreaming.

"Good girl," Maeve whispered. "So good for me."

Lolo gasped, half-awake now. Her legs parted instinctively.

Maeve kept her fingers light. Just enough to tease. Just enough to make Lolo arch without fully rising from sleep. She kissed up her belly again, over her sternum, her throat. "I've got you," she murmured. "You don't have to do anything. Just feel."

Lolo's eyes fluttered open.

She looked up at Maeve with a dazed, vulnerable kind of clarity.

Maeve smiled down at her.

Then kissed her softly.

"Stay still," she whispered.

## Chapter 14: Soft Reset

Lolo nodded. No words. Just breath.

Maeve slid down, positioning herself between her thighs. Her fingers returned—slick and steady now, stroking in slow, deliberate circles. Lolo gasped, her wrists twitching in the silk.

Maeve looked up. "You're gonna let me make you shake."

Lolo moaned.

"You're gonna come like this," Maeve said, voice low and full of worship. "Tied up and taken care of. No teasing. No punishment. Just me loving every inch of you."

She slipped two fingers inside, slow and deep.

Lolo cried out.

Maeve added her mouth.

Licked with precision. Fingers curling just right.

Lolo broke—body arching, voice gone, legs shaking as her orgasm hit like a wave and didn't stop. Maeve didn't stop. She held her there, coaxed another out, and another, until Lolo's thighs trembled and her belly fluttered under Maeve's hand.

Then Lolo gasped. Shuddered again. This time wetter. Harder. Her whole body tensed,and Maeve smiled against her, tasting it. Feeling it.

## Nail Me Down

"That's it," she whispered. "Let it go."

Lolo squirted—helpless, overwhelmed, undone.

Maeve held her.

Unwrapped her wrists with care.

When she finally pulled Lolo up into her lap, kissed her temple, and wrapped the blanket around them, Lolo just whispered, "I didn't know I could feel that much."

Maeve kissed her again. "You haven't even started."

Outside, the world stayed silent a little longer—just for them.

Maeve kept Lolo cradled in her arms, her back resting against Maeve's chest, breath slowing one exhale at a time. The blanket cocooned them both, but Maeve's hand remained pressed just above Lolo's heart, feeling the thrum of life still pulsing there like an echo of what they'd just shared. It made her throat tighten. Not with lust. With something gentler. Scarier.

She'd never been this soft with anyone before.

Not because she couldn't be. But because softness had always felt like surrender. Surrender of control, of silence, of herself had never been safe. But now it was different. Lolo had made it different.

Lolo shifted slightly, pressing her cheek to Maeve's shoulder.

## Chapter 14: Soft Reset

Her lashes were still damp, her lips slack with bliss. She looked wrung out and holy, and Maeve wondered *h I could live in this moment forever. I wouldn't need anything else.*

Neither of them spoke. The kind of quiet between them wasn't emptiness. It was full of knowing. Of breath and skin and unspoken yeses.

Maeve reached for Lolo's hand beneath the blanket and laced their fingers together. She could still feel the silk impressions on Lolo's wrist—faint, but present. Marks of trust. Of how freely Lolo had given herself.

"I didn't hurt you?" Maeve asked, voice low.

Lolo turned her head slightly. "Only in the best way."

Maeve smiled, but her jaw tensed. "I mean it. I need to know."

Lolo looked up then, eyes searching. She saw the real question behind Maeve's words. The vulnerability. The history. She squeezed her hand. "You held me the whole time. Even when I came apart. Especially then."

Maeve exhaled slowly. Relief, yes—but also something more complex. She wasn't used to being needed without also being feared. And Lolo? Lolo made needing feel like a shared act. Like a blueprint laid open on the table, just waiting to be followed.

"I want to do this right," Maeve said.

## Nail Me Down

"You already are," Lolo whispered.

They lay like that for a long time—touching without urgency, letting the aftershocks fade and the quiet bloom around them like dusk. Outside, the city stirred. A dog barked. Somewhere far below, a car alarm chirped once and went silent.

Maeve didn't care. The world could wait.

She leaned forward and pressed her lips to Lolo's temple. "We should stay in bed all day."

"We should," Lolo agreed, voice still thick with sleep and something sweeter.

"But we won't," Maeve said. "You'll stream. I'll measure framing for the Winston remodel. You'll make a joke about being sore. I'll roll my eyes. We'll flirt in the back room and act like no one notices."

Lolo grinned. "Because that's our rhythm."

Maeve nodded, fingers brushing down Lolo's side. "And because even when I'm not inside you… I'm still yours."

Lolo's smile faltered—not from fear, but from the weight of it. The truth. The steadiness.

She whispered back.

"Then I guess I'm home."

# Chapter 15: Hard Hat Heart

The housewarming wasn't fancy. But it was loud. Queer joy had a volume all its own, and in the restored brownstone, it rang out across three floors—glasses clinking, laughter spilling from the rooftop garden, a game of Cards Against Humanity derailing gloriously in the kitchen. The lights were low, music was high, and Maeve had already fixed a broken cabinet hinge once because someone tried to dance on it.

She didn't mind. It was her house. Their house.

Tonight, it was full of people who didn't flinch when they kissed. Who didn't blink when Lolo sat in her lap during dessert or when Maeve slipped a hand into the back of her hoodie and didn't move it. These were the friends they'd picked up in pieces—artists, streamers, welders, a trans bartender from the coffee place down the block, and a couple who taught queer youth how to box.

## Nail Me Down

It was the kind of home neither of them had ever imagined they'd get to build. But here it was—alive and warm.

Lolo was streaming from the reading nook Maeve had carved out near the bay window, her headset on, voice a purr as she thanked subscribers and showed off the party in chaotic snippets. She wore Maeve's hoodie. The big one. Faded black with paint stains on the sleeves and a stitched-over tear from when Maeve caught it on a scaffold hook. Lolo had rolled the sleeves up to her elbows, her thighs bare, one knee drawn to her chest as she winked at the camera.

"I live here now," she told chat. "With a woman who smells like cedar and judgment."

Maeve, from across the room, raised a brow.

"And she built me a bookshelf that doubles as a panic nook," Lolo added. "It's very sapphic of us."

Maeve didn't say anything. Just smiled to herself and walked back to the bedroom.

The party would carry on fine without her for ten minutes.

She stepped inside the room that had taken the longest to finish, not because of materials, but because of meaning. The bed sat low to the ground, framed in matte black steel she'd welded herself. The walls were painted a soft, bruised gray. The light from the string bulbs cast a golden wash across the ceiling.

## Chapter 15: Hard Hat Heart

She walked to the wall beam above the bed, the one she'd refused to drywall over.

She carved their initials into it.

Simple. Sharp.

M & L.

No hearts. No dates. Just fact.

She stepped back when she was done and exhaled. Then touched the letters with the tips of her fingers. She didn't say anything out loud. But the silence felt full, like it had heard her anyway.

Behind her, footsteps.

Lolo.

She was barefoot now. Hoodie still on. Headset gone.

She stepped beside Maeve, looked at the beam, and said nothing for a long time.

Then she pulled up her hoodie just enough to show her new tattoo.

It was small. Sharp. Placed on her hip just where Maeve's palm always curled when they slept.

## Nail Me Down

A chisel.

Delicate. Intimate. Undeniably hers.

Maeve swallowed. She hadn't known.

Lolo looked up at her. "You build everything," she said. "So I wanted to carry a piece of it."

Maeve stared at the tattoo like it was sacred. Like it might vanish if she blinked too hard. Then she dropped to her knees and kissed it.

Not with heat.

With worship.

Lolo's breath hitched. Her fingers curled in Maeve's hair.

Neither of them moved for a long time.

Later, long after the guests had left and the rooftop had gone quiet, they lay together under a mess of blankets. Lolo was tucked against Maeve's side, the hoodie discarded, skin warm and still humming. Maeve traced the tattoo with her lips once more.

"You're mine," she whispered.

Lolo smiled without opening her eyes. "Only always."

## Chapter 15: Hard Hat Heart

Every night after that, Maeve kissed the tattoo before they slept. She never missed a night.

Because some rituals weren't loud.

They were steady.

Like construction.

Like love.

Like a hard hat heart.

It wasn't flashy. It didn't announce itself. It didn't scream through the cracks of drama or demand a spotlight. Maeve's love was made of bolts and weather-sealed plans, of tiny adjustments at the baseboard and screws tightened under pressure. But it held. It held through mornings when words failed and nights when Lolo cried and didn't know why. It held when the heater clicked wrong or the faucet dripped at 2 A.M.. Maeve fixed those things without needing thanks. She just did.

Every night—without exception—Maeve leaned over Lolo's sleeping form and pressed her lips to the inked outline of the chisel carved onto her hip. Not because it was expected. Because it was true. Because ritual wasn't about performance. It was about presence.

Lolo never stopped noticing. Even if her eyes were closed, her breath slowed, her mind floating between dreams and memory, she always felt it. That kiss. That mark. That promise.

## Nail Me Down

They learned to live in the space between noise and quiet. Lolo's days remained loud, full of laughter and streams and chaotic edits and clinking mugs of coffee on coasters Maeve had made from reclaimed tile. Maeve's life hummed with precision—calloused hands, steel frames, the deep hum of power tools, schedules, and sawdust caught in the cuffs of her jeans. They were opposites. But not really. They were matched. Like studs and drywall. Like warmth and weight.

On Sundays, they didn't leave the house.

Maeve made pancakes. Lolo stole half the batter. They kissed in doorways, tangled on the living room floor, read each other passages from books that neither of them had the patience to finish. They argued over whether the spice rack should be alphabetical or chaotic queer energy. Maeve carved out little storage solutions under the stairs. Lolo hid love notes in all of them.

When one of them couldn't speak—too tired, too wound up, too human—the other made space without question. Maeve held Lolo's feet in her lap while she cried through a bad stream day. Lolo sat behind Maeve in the workshop and braided her hair while she reworked a project for the third time.

They didn't say forever. They said next. As in: What's next?

Because love wasn't a finish line. It was a process. A patch. A reset. A reinforcement.

Maeve didn't write poetry, but she left her initials on every

## Chapter 15: Hard Hat Heart

corner beam she laid, like a signature the world could never erase. Lolo didn't always trust quiet, but she trusted Maeve's.

When storms came—and they did—they weathered them. Maeve anchored. Lolo lit candles. They met in the middle, over and over, in doorways and kitchen counters and the softness of shared bedsheets that smelled like rosemary and sweat and lavender.

Some nights, Maeve caught herself staring—not at Lolo's curves or smile, though she loved both—but at the way she existed. Fully. Honestly. Without apology.

She'd kiss the tattoo, whisper nothing, and fall asleep with her arm over the woman who had once made her feel too much and now made her feel enough.

Hard hat hearts weren't soft. But they were real.

They held.

# Epilogue — Glitched and Glorious

Lolo's channel had blown up months ago.

It started with a clip—a rogue bit of stream chaos where she spilled tea on her keyboard mid-monologue about emotional bandwidth in cozy games, then casually transitioned into reading thirst tweets about her "contractor girlfriend with terrifying forearms." The video went viral. She didn't mean for it to. But when her subscriber count tripled and someone on Twitter called them "The Queerest Final Boss Couple on Twitch," she leaned into it.

Not for the fame.

For the platform. For the joy. For the weirdos like her who needed to see softness wrapped in snark and see a woman with a body like hers be loved like religion. She streamed twice a week now—variety gaming, DIY fails, makeup tutorials done in power tools lighting. And always, always in one of Maeve's

## Epilogue — Glitched and Glorious

hoodies.

Her chat knew it. Called it the Contractor Collection. Maeve had said nothing about it the first dozen times. But after Lolo threw one on backward during a late-night stream and deadpanned "Daddy's gear comes pre-wrecked," Maeve started labeling the hoodies with their own color-coded drawer system.

Because Maeve didn't joke online. She just built.

Her firm had tripled in size.

Not in staff, but in scope. She didn't just do luxury remodels anymore. She became known for something else—something more needed. Kink-safe renovations. Queer-informed build-outs. Homes with reinforced beams for suspensions. Discreet bondage shelving. Shower rails that doubled as restraint points. Flooring that held. Soundproofing that didn't judge. Spaces that were private, yes, but also sacred.

Clients came in nervous. Left with blueprints they didn't know how to ask for until Maeve handed them over like they were obvious.

It wasn't just design. It was devotion.

Their home held the rhythm of both their lives now.

The living room always smelled like lavender, old pine, and want. Candles burned down half-drunk. Velvet throws lay tangled under stacks of notes. Lolo's headphones hung from a wall hook beside Maeve's carpenter belt. They didn't keep separate spaces anymore. They didn't need to.

Every room bore signs of both of them.

The chisel tattoo still lived on Lolo's hip. Maeve still kissed it every night. She'd added a new habit: pressing her palm to it first, holding it like proof. Like grounding.

They didn't say forever. They didn't have to.

Instead, they built things.

Breakfast routines. Stream schedules. Maeve learned to tolerate ring lights in the bedroom. Lolo stopped reorganizing the tool wall by color. They fought about grout once and then had makeup sex that cracked the plaster behind the bed. They left it that way. Marked. Imperfect. Theirs.

Some nights, Maeve watched Lolo from the hallway—headphones on, eyes bright, her voice full of bite and delight. She never interrupted. But sometimes, she left things beside the streaming nook. A glass of ginger tea, a favorite hoodie, a handwritten note that simply said 'Go wreck them, baby'.

Other nights, Lolo wandered into the workshop at midnight and curled up on the floor next to Maeve's bench, half-asleep and smiling.

"You gonna install aftercare shelving in every unit now?" she mumbled once.

## Epilogue — Glitched and Glorious

Maeve didn't look up. "Every single one."

They'd become a myth in their friend circle. The Dom who brought you reclaimed wood. The brat who got partnerships with three indie devs and designed stickers shaped like impact toys. They were chaos and order. Joke and jawline. Blueprint and glitter.

Once, Lolo invited Maeve onto a stream for a 'build-your-own bookshelf' segment.

Maeve lasted twenty minutes.

She didn't speak to the camera once. Just tightened screws, handed tools, and made Lolo breathless when she whispered good girl off-mic.

The chat went feral.

Maeve built the shelf anyway. It still stood behind Lolo's chair. Every time it creaked on stream, someone donated.

Lolo tattooed a second piece later. This one on her ribs. A simple etching of a stud wall, faint text beneath it: She held me up before I knew I needed support.

Maeve didn't speak for a long time after seeing it.

Then she carved Lolo's channel logo into the frame of their bedroom beam—hidden behind the molding. Lolo found it six months later. Cried for half an hour.

## Nail Me Down

They didn't chase dreams. They crafted them.

Measured. Sanded. Screwed into place. Adjusted. Re-braced. Real.

They made love in between toolboxes and thumbnail edits. They fought about nothing. They made up over pizza and Post-its. They hosted brunches where half the guests had calluses and the other half had eyeliner wings like blades.

It wasn't perfect.

But it held.

Because in the end, they didn't need forever.

They had each other.

One build at a time.

Maeve learned that love didn't come with schematics. There was no master plan, no perfect angle. Sometimes, you had to tear down load-bearing lies to find where the truth could stand. Sometimes, you measured wrong. Sometimes, the studs weren't where you expected. But with Lolo, Maeve kept building anyway. Kept showing up with her tools and her silence and her steadiness. And Lolo kept opening the door.

Their life didn't look like anyone else's. It wasn't supposed to.

Lolo's mornings were slow and saccharine, full of mug-warmed honey, custom playlist curation, and chat polls about what kind

## Epilogue — Glitched and Glorious

of slippers were the gayest. Maeve's started at dawn, usually with her nose buried in insulation invoices, trying not to spill coffee on blueprints. But around 10 a.m., like clockwork, Maeve would slide behind Lolo midstream, set down something gentle a hot drink, a cooling pack, a fresh shirt—and press her lips to the top of her head without a word.

Her chat loved it. Lolo pretended to be annoyed. Maeve never broke stride.

They'd built a calendar together. Not for dates or deadlines, but for each other. Sunday mornings were for being horizontal. Wednesdays meant lunch in the garden. Every full moon, Lolo lit incense in the workshop while Maeve polished her chisels. Neither of them believed in cosmic ritual. But they believed in showing up. And sometimes, that was magic enough.

They got used to the odd rhythm of queer success. Lolo had an editor now. Maeve had two new apprentices. Sometimes they didn't see each other until late at night, when one crawled into bed and found the other already dreaming. But the kiss was always there. So was the chisel tattoo. So was the weight of shared air.

Maeve never said "I love you" in the ways people expected.

She said it in motion. In rebuilt door frames. In the fact that she installed three new outlets under Lolo's desk because she noticed the cord tangle stressed her out. She said it in the way she knotted silk ribbon just tight enough around Lolo's wrists and in how she washed her hands after—gently, carefully, like

## *Nail Me Down*

Lolo's pleasure lived under her fingernails.

Lolo said it louder. Through declarations and chaos. Through her laugh when Maeve cracked her neck after carrying lumber, and through the 'babe, don't touch that, I'm filming!' at least twice a week. But she also said it in whispers. In the way she cleaned Maeve's brushes. In the notes she left in her boots.

They made love like they built everything else—responsive, layered, unfinished in the best way.

Some nights were soft resets: Lolo tied to the bedpost with nothing but her breath in her throat and Maeve's praise on loop. Other nights were demolition: teeth, sweat, drywall dust in their hair. Every version was real. Every version was them.

They didn't agree on everything.

Lolo still hated structural symmetry. Maeve still alphabetized their spice rack. But they held each disagreement like a temporary project—something that would settle into place eventually, given enough trust and time.

They kept learning.

How to be better at listening. How to fall into silence without making it a weapon. How to admit when they were scared. How to come home angry and still hold hands in bed. How to grieve. How to grow.

Lolo started teaching workshops—digital spaces for queer

## Epilogue — Glitched and Glorious

intimacy, kink safety, communication skills. Maeve sat in on one once. Just listened. Didn't say a word. But Lolo saw her in the attendee list and smiled so wide her mod had to mute her for thirty seconds.

Maevewas asked to speak at a panel about gendered labor and trades. She brought Lolo with her. She didn't talk much. But when she said, "I build homes for people like us," the room went still.

They weren't just partners. They were proof.

Proof that a queer life didn't have to be tragedy or fight. It could be sawdust and live-stream chaos. It could be silk rope and grilled cheese. It could be tattoos and tax deductions. It could be laughter that echoed and silence that healed.

It never stopped evolving.

Not toward perfection. But toward honesty.

They didn't need a white dress moment or a ring.

They had steel and ink. They had breath and blueprint. They had each other.

One build at a time. Every day. Forever by choice—not promise.

Glitched and glorious. Just like them.

*Nail Me Down*

www.ingramcontent.com/pod-product-compliance
Lightning Source LLC
LaVergne TN
LVHW091741300525
812593LV00001B/136